Broomstick Services

"Don't be silly, Lucy. They're not witches. They're just trying to scare us. Let's go and tell the head."

Mabel leapt up and, holding her hands out, shouted:

*"Little children! In a trice,
You will all be furry mice."*

"No, Mabel," cried Ethel, looking at the three mice running around the floor of the shed, "not mice. Remember we've got Black Cat with us."

ANN JUNGMAN

Broomstick Services

Illustrated by Jan Lewis

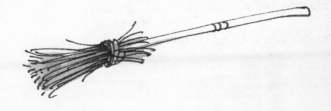

Hippo

For Margaret Barbalet with love

Scholastic Children's Books,
Scholastic Publications Ltd,
7–9 Pratt Street, London NW1 0AE, UK

Scholastic Inc.,
555 Broadway, New York, NY 10012-3999, USA

Scholastic Canada Ltd,
123 Newkirk Road, Richmond Hill,
Ontario, Canada L4C 3G5

Ashton Scholastic Pty Ltd,
P O Box 579, Gosford, New South Wales,
Australia

Ashton Scholastic Ltd,
Private Bag 92801, Penrose, Auckland,
New Zealand

First published in 1990 by Scholastic Publications Ltd
This edition, 1995

Text copyright © Ann Jungman, 1990
Illustrations copyright © Jan Lewis, 1995

ISBN 0 590 13174 5

Typeset by Contour Typesetters, Southall, London
Printed by Cox & Wyman Ltd, Reading, Berks

10 9 8 7 6 5 4 3 2 1

Chapter One

In the Car Park

On the outskirts of the town stood a brand new supermarket, surrounded by a huge concrete car park. During the day the car park bustled with busy shoppers but at night it was completely empty. Well, that was usually the case, but one dark November night anyone passing would have been surprised to see the most amazing sight.

In a little cluster of trees on one side of the car park were three witches, dancing round a cauldron. As they kicked their legs up in the air they sang at the tops of their voices:

"Bubble, bubble, toil and trouble,
Fire burn and cauldron bubble."

On a branch of one of the trees sat a black cat, howling in tune with the witches and waving his tail happily. After a while they stopped singing and dancing and sat round the fire.

"Let's think of something really wicked to do tonight," said the tallest witch, smiling in the moonlight.

"Something really horrible to punish those people who dared to build a car park on our sacred site."

"It's not that bad, Maud," said the smallest of the witches. "They weren't to know that this was our sacred site, and at least our special tree is still here."

"Not that bad?" spat out the tall witch. "Honestly, Ethel, I despair of you, I really do. Things are getting worse and worse for us witches. The twentieth century has been a disaster. When we were young we were always bumping into other witches on their

broomsticks. Now you never see anyone. I haven't had a broomstick crash
for years. Soon it will be impossible to
make any spells at all. And all you can
do is make excuses for people. Now
come on, both of you, help me think up
a terrible and suitable revenge."

"We could make all the lights go
out," suggested the third witch, a
plump and jolly figure.

"Yes!" agreed Ethel. "They wouldn't
like that one bit. And make all the
televisions go off."

"And the heating," continued the plump witch, "and the electric blankets and the washing-machines and the videos and the computers and all the funny gadgets that people have in their houses these days."

"You're hopeless, absolutely hopeless, the pair of you," fumed the tall witch. "Thank goodness poor dear Mother isn't here to listen to the pathetic suggestions you're making. Now stop messing around and help me think of something really bad, really mean and horrible."

"Oh, Maud," sighed the plump witch, "you're such a dreamer. Why can't you just accept that witches have had it? We just don't fit any more – in this world full of supermarkets and

televisions and cars and walkmans. We're as old-fashioned as corsets and lavender and cucumber sandwiches, and I for one have had enough."

"Enough?" thundered Maud. "You miserable bat-faced apology for a witch! What do you mean you've had enough? Mabel, I demand an explanation."

"I've had enough of being a witch in the last part of the twentieth century and so I've decided to give it up. I'm going to be ordinary."

"Ordinary?" shrieked Maud. "What is that supposed to mean, you great soggy bag of mashed potatoes?"

Mabel flushed but looked hard into Maud's flashing eyes.

"What I mean, Maud, is that I'm going off into the world and I'm going to try and find a job and live like an ordinary person. I don't want to spend my time dancing round an old pot and riding around on an old broomstick, thinking up silly spells. I know when I'm beaten. No more witchery for me."

"Good!" shouted Maud. "You go then, and try and become an ordinary person. You'll soon find out what it's like out there. They won't want to know you. You'll be cold and lonely and hungry, but don't think Ethel and I will hang around waiting for you to come to your senses. We'll be off to some distant place and you may not be able to find us. Isn't that right, Ethel?"

"Well, actually, Maud," whispered Ethel, biting her nails and looking at the ground, "I think I'd like to go with Mabel. I'm tired of being a witch too."

"Worms, traitors, miserable toads!" thundered Maud. "Well, off you both go then, but I'm keeping the cauldron and the book of spells. I may be the last wicked witch left in the world, but I shall never desert the old ways of our mother and grandmother and the generations before them. I shall continue with our great ways till the end of time."

"Each to her own taste, Maud," said Mabel cheerfully. "We're very happy for you to keep the cauldron and the book of spells. Ethel and I will have no need of such things where we are going. Now, Maud dear, take good care of yourself and don't forget to wear your warmest knickers when the weather gets worse. You could catch your death of cold flying around up there. I do hope that when Ethel and I are settled you will come and visit us. We don't want to lose touch. I mean, we are still sisters, even if we have chosen different paths."

"Don't be ridiculous," yelled Maud. "I wouldn't lower myself by talking to creeps like you. Don't think you'll get away with this, because you won't.

You'll come crawling back to me begging for forgiveness and, who knows, maybe I'll be in a good mood and help, or then again maybe I won't."

"Oh, dear," sighed Mabel. "I had hoped we'd manage an agreeable parting of the ways. Still, if you won't have it you won't. Well, our door will always be open to you, Maud, and I wish you well."

"Me, too," whispered Ethel. "And do please come to see us, Maud. I'd be so sad never to see you again."

With a last glance at Maud, Ethel and Mabel walked off hand in hand, down the road that led to the town. Mabel heard a little squeak as she strode off and when she looked down she saw their black cat running along beside them.

"Look, Ethel," she said happily, "Black Cat has decided to come with us."

As they walked away carrying their broomsticks, they could hear Maud behind them singing loudly:

"By toad in ditch and owl in tree,
Curses on those who abandon me."

"Can you hear that, Mabel?" whispered Ethel.

"Of course I can. She is fierce, isn't she? Still, courage, Ethel, courage. We had to do it and I expect Maud will come round eventually."

"I expect you're right, Mabel. I'm so tired I can't even think straight."

"What we need is some sleep," agreed Mabel. "Tomorrow we can plan our new life, when we feel fresh and it's daylight. Let's find somewhere to sleep."

"There's a hut over there."

"I can't read what it says on the board outside. We'll have to make some light. Come on, Ethel, there's no one around. Let's see if we can make the light spell work. Black

16

Cat, you help too."

So the two witches raised their hands to the sky and chanted:

"By raven's toe and magpie's hoard,
Let light shine on yonder board."

Black Cat howled into the darkness in support.

A flash of lightning came out of nowhere and lit up the board.

"It worked," said Ethel proudly, cheering up a little.

"Yes," agreed Mabel, "and it says 'St Margaret's Primary School'. Well, that's good. Schools are empty at night. Come on, Ethel, we'll sleep in that hut and by the time the children come to school, we'll be well away."

"Are you sure it's safe, Mabel?"

"Don't be so wet, Ethel. Of course it's safe. Now come on, on to your broomstick and we'll just hop over the railings. One, two, three. Jump on, Black Cat, and over we go."

And within five minutes both the witches were fast asleep in the hut where the school caretaker kept his tools.

Chapter Two

In the Playground

The next day the children came to school as usual and played until the bell went for lessons to begin. The witches slept through it all. Playtime came and still the two witches slept. However, Black Cat, feeling bored and hungry, squeezed through a hole in the wall and began to walk round the playground. A group of children stopped playing ball and ran over to the cat.

"Look, a cat. Puss, puss, come here, puss, puss, puss," said Lucy, kneeling down to stroke him.

Black Cat didn't like children and he raced back to the hut as fast as he could. The three children followed.

"It's gone into the caretaker's hut," yelled Joe.

"We must have scared it," said Jackie. "Let's go and see if it wants some milk."

The children pulled the door of the hut open and there, snoring away, surrounded by spades and rakes and buckets, lay Mabel and Ethel. The sudden light and draught woke the two

witches, who sat up and looked round at their unusual surroundings, blinking and rubbing their eyes. The children looked at the witches and the witches looked at the children. The children couldn't believe their eyes.

"Well, come in," said Mabel eventually. "It's cold with the door open."

The children stepped inside and Joe shut the door behind them.

"You look like witches," he said in amazement.

"We are witches," Mabel told him. "But we're not the bad kind, well, not any more we're not."

21

"I'm not scared," said Lucy. "They're not witches. They're just trying to scare us. Let's go and tell the head."

Mabel leapt up and, holding her hands out, shouted:

"Little children! In a trice
You will all be furry mice."

"No, Mabel," cried Ethel, looking at the three mice running around on the floor of the shed, "not mice. Remember we've got Black Cat with us."

Black Cat was crouching and arching his back, preparing to leap on the mice.

"Little cat with coat so black,
From now on you will be a – a – coat
*   rack."*

A second later, there in the tumble-down hut, stood a lovely, shiny wooden coat rack.

"Now you turn those children back into themselves," said Ethel in an angry voice. "Honestly, Mabel, that was more like Maud than you. Remember we're supposed to be changing our ways."

"Sorry, Ethel," said Mabel, sitting down. "I just didn't think. They gave me a shock and I did the first thing that came into my head. Right, what is the spell to turn mice into children? Oh dear, Ethel, I've forgotten it."

Ethel shut her eyes and thought. Then she cried:

"*Little mice, one, two, three,*
Once again children be."

But the children went on being mice.
"It didn't work! Oh, Mabel, think hard."
Mabel burst out:

"*You three funny mice*
Be children sweet and nice."

But still nothing happened. "Oh, no, they're still mice. Try again, Ethel."

"Don't worry. I'm sure I've got it this time," said Ethel.

"You three furry, squeaky mice,
Be once more children in a trice."

Suddenly Joe, Lucy and Jackie stood in front of them again.

"I'm very sorry," began Mabel to the children. "I just wasn't thinking."

"No, we were asleep, you see," added Ethel. "You had better report us now, we've asked for it."

"You *are* witches!" burst out Jackie. "You really, really are!"

"That's right," said Mabel. "Now, come on, let's get it over with. Take us to the head, or whoever you think is the right person."

"You can't be bad witches," said Lucy. "If you had been you'd have let that cat eat us and escaped."

"What are you doing here, anyway?" demanded Jackie.

So Mabel explained about the quarrel with Maud and how she and Ethel had had enough.

"So, you see," said Mabel, "we want to be ordinary and the first thing we need to do is find a way to earn a bit of money, so that we can buy food. Can you help us?"

"Why should they help us, Mabel?" demanded Ethel. "If you'd turned me into a mouse with a cat nearby, I wouldn't want to help you."

"I'd like to help," said Joe. "This is the most exciting thing that's happened to me for ages."

"Yes," agreed Jackie. "Once the cat had been turned into a coat rack I enjoyed being a mouse."

Just then the bell for the end of playtime went but the children didn't want to go back to their classrooms.

"We must go," Jackie pointed out,

"or everyone will come looking for us and they'll find Mabel and Ethel. You two stay here. We'll bring you some food at lunchtime, and after school we'll have another talk and try to think of a way out of your problem."

The Great Idea

As soon as school was over the children put their money together and bought some crisps and juice for the witches and some milk for Black Cat (for when he stopped being a coat rack) and raced over to the hut. While they sat round munching, they tried to think what the witches could do to earn money.

"You could sweep the streets with your broomsticks," suggested Joe.

"That won't do," replied Jackie. "They clean the streets with machines these days."

"You could sweep the leaves in the park in autumn," suggested Lucy.

"Yes," sniffed Mabel, "but what would we do the rest of the year?"

Jackie suddenly jumped up.

"I have a brilliant idea," she cried.

"All right, genius, let's hear it," said Joe.

"The broomsticks, do they work?" asked Jackie.

"Of course they do," said Ethel indignantly. "I mean we are witches after all, even if we do want to be like ordinary people."

"Good," said Jackie. "Then you could deliver to people living high up in tower blocks."

"What are you on about, genius?" asked Lucy.

"You know what it's like in those high tower blocks. The lifts are always broken. People like my gran like to have fish and chips and things, but they don't want to walk down fifteen flights of stairs and then up again. Ethel and Mabel could deliver food through the windows."

"It's a great idea," said Joe. "Congratulations, Jackie, I'd never have thought of it."

"Yeah," agreed Lucy, "it's something that only someone who could ride a broomstick could do. It could be a real service."

"There is a problem," Joe pointed out. "Most people don't believe in witches and they won't take the idea seriously."

"That's true," agreed Mabel sadly, "and there are some who don't like us. They'd call the police in no time."

"I know what we have to do," cried Jackie. "We have to talk to my gran."

"What's your gran got to do with it?" asked Joe.

"She's the Chairperson of the Senior Citizens' Association and the Tenants' Association. That means she knows everyone who lives in the flats. If we could get her on our side, she could persuade all the others to give Ethel and Mabel a fair chance."

"I like your gran," said Joe. "She listens to us. Let's all go round and see if we can get her to agree to help."

"Yes, let's," agreed Lucy. "But, Ethel and Mabel, you must leave your hats and broomsticks here. Hang them on the coat rack. We don't want to give Jackie's gran a shock. We want her to get used to the idea slowly."

Reluctantly the witches agreed. They left their hats and brooms behind and followed the children to the block of flats. As the lift was broken they had to walk up fifteen flights.

"I can see why they'd want us to deliver to them," panted Mabel. "These stairs are terrible."

When they finally got to Jackie's gran's flat, they all trooped in.

"Hello, Jackie love. Hello, Joe and Lucy," said Gran. "Nice to see you. And who are these two ladies? I don't think I've ever met you before."

"No, you haven't. I'm Mabel and this is my sister, Ethel."

"Well, sit down. I'll make us a nice cup of tea. You all look very tired."

While they sat drinking their tea Ethel and Mabel looked round curiously.

"So this is how people live," said Ethel. "Very nice."

"What an odd thing to say," said Gran, looking puzzled. "Whatever do you mean?"

"It's what we came to see you about, Gran," burst out Jackie. "You see we need your help very, very much."

"My help! Whatever for?"

"It's for Mabel and Ethel. You see they're both witches but they want to find work and earn a living, and we want to help them. Now, I've had this brilliant idea that they should deliver food and things on their broomsticks to people in the flats. I thought that if you agreed to explain to all the people who live in the flats, it might work."

"Just a minute. Are you trying to tell me these two ladies are witches?"

"Yes, we are witches," Mabel told her, "or at least we *were*."

"Don't be silly," said Gran. "Everyone knows witches don't exist. Is this some kind of a joke?"

"No, honestly," said Ethel. "We are witches, but good ones and we want to use our special abilities, like riding broomsticks, to help people and earn a living."

Gran burst out laughing.

"You're all playing a joke on me. Well, I like a good laugh. Pity it's not true. Having people to deliver food and shopping and laundry and things through the window would be wonderful. Nice idea."

"But it could come true," Ethel told her. "Honestly. Now listen, if we fly up to your window with your supper all hot and ready to eat, would you believe us?"

"I'd have to," laughed Gran.

"Right, let's have your order and off we go."

"I don't believe you can do it, but all right. I'll have a pizza. Here's some money. Buy three large ones. Jackie's Uncle Fred will be here soon and we can all share them for tea."

They all rushed back to the school and rescued the broomsticks and hats, and Ethel turned the coat rack back into Black Cat so that he could have his milk. Then they walked quickly to Pizza Hut and the children bought three different pizzas and handed them to Ethel and Mabel. The two witches flew as fast as they could to the block of flats.

Gran stood at her window, looking out with interest. At that moment Uncle Fred arrived. Gran quickly explained what was happening and Uncle Fred joined her at the window. When they saw the two witches on their broomsticks flying towards them, they couldn't believe their eyes.

"Three piping hot pizzas for number 273," said Mabel.

Eventually Gran found her voice.

"And they are piping hot too. Well, you'd better come in and we'll have a talk while we eat."

"We'll just fetch the children and then we'll be with you in two ticks."

To Uncle Fred's amazement, the children were soon sitting on the broomsticks and flying through the air with shrieks of excitement. He had to pinch himself to make sure he wasn't dreaming as Ethel, Mabel and the children flew through the window. Gran introduced the witches to Uncle Fred, and a few minutes later they were sitting round, drinking tea and eating slices of pizza. Everyone agreed that it looked as though Broomstick Services would go down very well.

"I think we should get it off to a flying start," said Joe.

Everyone groaned at the pun.

"No, seriously," he said. "We should have a grand opening night. Send out notices to everyone in the flats and then put on a big show, you know, music and lights, get it in the local paper, and everything. That way everyone in the area would get to know about Mabel and Ethel and they'd be busy every night."

"It's a smashing idea," said Mabel. "You are clever children. We were jolly lucky to meet you. We'd never have thought of all this on our own."

"Let's design a card now," said Gran.

"Let's see, what should it say? How about:

Is your lift always broken? Do you hate walking up hundreds of stairs? Is the shopping too heavy? Is the take-away always cold when you get it home? Now your problems are solved. Broomstick Services will bring you fast food or shopping to your very window. Fast, clean, efficient, reliable and cheap service. First orders taken on Friday night at 7 p.m. Don't miss this rare opportunity. BE AT YOUR WINDOWS. Free delivery on Friday night only."

"Sounds great," said Lucy. "Now we'll all have to work very hard writing these out. Then we'll have to deliver them before Friday."

"Ethel and I could do the cards," said Mabel. "If we had somewhere to stay we could do them all day and decorate them with hats and broomsticks and things."

"You can stay here," Gran offered. "It'll be a bit cramped but I like company. You're very welcome."

"Thanks," said Mabel. "We'd love to."

"Maud was so wrong," muttered Ethel. "She said no one would want us but so far everyone has been so kind. I'd have given up being a witch years ago if I'd known."

Chapter Four

The Opening Night

Gran called meetings of the Senior Citizens' and the Tenants' Associations and told them all about the wonderful service that Mabel and Ethel were offering. Some people had doubts about allowing witches on to the estate but Gran assured them that Ethel and

Mabel had definitely decided to give up doing wicked things and that their special skills would only be used to help people. Eventually it was agreed to give the witches one chance on the following Friday.

When Friday night came, everything was ready. Joe had borrowed as many tape recorders as he could and had recorded the rousing music of *The William Tell Overture* to accompany the opening flight. Lucy had gone round the flats and persuaded everyone to put their lights on at seven o'clock.

As seven o'clock approached, most of the people who lived in the flats were leaning out of their windows waiting to see what would happen. Mabel and Ethel brushed their long black locks and

put on their tall, shiny black hats.

"Five minutes to go," said Jackie. "Are you nervous?"

"Not me," said Mabel. "I'm looking forward to it. Fame at last."

Suddenly they heard a scream from Ethel.

"Ethel," said Mabel sternly, "pull yourself together. I won't tolerate a show of nerves at this stage, just when everyone has been so helpful."

"Our broomsticks," Ethel burst out. "Look, they've gone."

"Oh, no," groaned Mabel.

"What are we going to do?" demanded Joe. "Everyone is waiting."

"Maud, it must be Maud," exclaimed Mabel. "I wondered when she'd strike. Of all the low-down tricks."

Above them they heard a loud cackle. They looked up and there was Maud, her hair flowing in the wind, hovering on her broomstick overhead and clutching their broomsticks.

"What did you expect, dear sisters? I'm still a wicked witch. Did you expect fair play? You're even softer than I thought. Well, try and launch your little scheme now. See how much your new friends will like you when you let them down."

"Maud, you come here this minute and bring our broomsticks back."

"Never," yelled Maud defiantly. "I won't let you use witch magic to help people.

By toad in ditch and owl in tree,
Curses on those who challenge me."

51

And she flew off into the darkness, laughing loudly.

"Do something," yelled Joe. "There are only a couple of minutes to go. Everyone is waiting."

"Couldn't you magic some ordinary brooms or something?" said Lucy. "I mean, you're witches. Do they have to be the special twiggy kind of broomsticks?"

"I don't know," said Mabel. "I mean, it's never come up before. Get me a couple of brooms and we'll have a go."

The children rushed off.

"I knew something would happen to spoil it all," moaned Ethel.

"Be quiet," said Mabel firmly, "and start thinking about spells to magic brooms. All is not yet lost. We can still

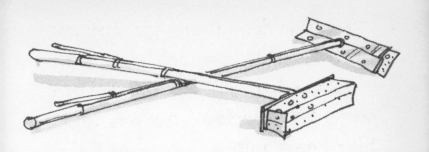

show Maud a thing or two."

A few moments later the children returned clutching two squeegy mops.

"What on earth are those?" demanded Mabel.

"Squeegy mops. They're for cleaning floors too. They were the nearest thing we could find in a hurry. Will they do?"

"We'll have to give it a try," sighed Mabel.

"Well, hurry up. It's after seven o'clock and people are getting impatient."

All over the flats people were leaning

out of their windows shouting, "Why are we waiting?"

"Can you think of a spell, Mabel?" asked Ethel. "They've all gone clean out of my head. Maud always looked after the broomsticks and she's got the Magic Book."

"I'm going to try. Now quiet, everyone. Here we go:

Squeegy mop so bright and clean,
Hover now in the moon's beam.
Fly up, fly up, fly up so high,
Into the cold winter night sky."

They all looked hopefully at the squeegy mops. But nothing happened.

The cries of "Why are we waiting?" got louder.

Then Ethel burst out:

"I remember! I remember now! It only works if we do it standing on our heads. Come on, Mabel, not a moment to lose. One, two, three and upside down."

From the upside-down position the two witches repeated the spell. The children watched with bated breath. The two mops began to fly up into the air.

"Wait for us," yelled the two witches as they quickly stood up.

"They've got away," cried Jackie. "Get them back. You've got to get them back."

"*By witch's nose and giant's knee, I order you mops to return to me*," cried Ethel desperately.

The two mops came crashing down, sending the little group flying and knocking Mabel over.

"Well done, Ethel," said the children. "Now quick, we'll start the music and you can begin the real business of the evening."

"Come on, Mabel," Ethel told her sister. "No point in lying there in the mud. We've got work to do."

"Right," agreed Mabel, staggering to her feet and grabbing the mop firmly. "Come on, Black Cat, up you get behind."

But Black Cat hunched his back and hissed and, waving his tail, walked away.

"He won't come," said Mabel sadly. "He must think it would be undignified."

"Don't worry," said Lucy. "You don't really need him to fly with you, not tonight."

"Music starting on the count of three," shouted Joe. "One, two, three."

As the music blared out, the two witches rose in the air on the mops. A great cheer went up, as they flew round waving their hats in the air and blowing kisses. Then Ethel began taking orders and Mabel flew off to the various shops and restaurants to collect the food.

"Chicken for Mrs Barzetti," called Ethel. "Two kingsize hamburgers for the Brown twins, and sweet and sour pork for Mr Griffin at number 49."

All evening the witches flew around delivering piping hot food, chatting merrily to all their customers and finally taking away the empty cartons and putting them neatly in the dustbins.

When it was all over, everyone agreed that it had been a huge success and promised to use the witches' services on a regular basis and recommend them to their friends. That night Mabel and Ethel collapsed in Gran's flat, exhausted but happy.

"We did it, Ethel. We made it. We've got a job."

"I know," agreed her sister, "and we're making friends too. Maud couldn't have been more wrong."

"Poor old Maud," mused Mabel. "I wonder how long she'll keep it up. With a bit of luck she'll see how well we're doing and join us. It would be nice for the three of us to be together again, and Black Cat too. I wonder where he went."

"We'll just have to hope he turns up," said Ethel. "Now go to sleep. Tomorrow is going to be another hard-working day for Broomstick Services."

Chapter Five

Maud Joins In

Ethel and Mabel were a huge success. Every day they made flights to do people's shopping, to take washing to the laundrette, to collect medicines from the chemist and even to entertain children when they were bored. After a few weeks they were offered a flat on the thirty-fifth floor, which no one wanted because it was too high up. The two witches were thrilled to bits and busily set about painting it. When that was done, they went out and bought some pieces of secondhand furniture and a television.

"Fancy us having a place of our own, Mabel," said Ethel happily. "I wonder what Maud would say if she could see us now."

"I hope she's all right," answered Mabel. "It's a cold winter. I wish we could have sent her a change-of-address card but we don't know where to find her."

"She found us when she wanted to be mean to us," Ethel pointed out. "She'll find us if she needs us. Would you like

another cup of tea, Mabel dear? There's
a good film on the television starting in
a few minutes."

So the witches sat drinking tea and
watching television and enjoying the
warmth and cosiness of their own
home. They were just about to turn the
television off, when they heard a knock
on the window.

"Must be the wind," said Mabel.

"Must be," agreed Ethel.

But the knocking went on. The
sisters looked at each other. Then they
heard a cat miaowing.

"It is! It must be! It's Maud and Black Cat," cried Ethel, pulling back the curtain, and there, hovering on her broomstick, was their sister.

"Come on in," cried Mabel, opening the window. Maud flew in, wet and shivering.

"You need a hot bath," declared Ethel. "Come on, Maud, come and see our lovely bathroom."

Rather to Mabel's surprise, Maud allowed herself to be led to the bath-room and put into a steaming bubble bath. Mabel quickly heated up some soup and when Maud emerged, she was seated in front of the fire and given the soup. Black Cat, who was skinny, wet and miserable, was given food too.

"How did you find us?" asked Ethel.

"I've been trying to find you for ages. It was lonely without you. Being wicked was no fun on my own. So I said to Black Cat here, let's go and find them, and we did."

"We've done very well since we left, as you can see. We've got good work, a lovely place to live and lots of friends. Now, what do you say to that?"

"All right, I was mistaken. There's no need to rub it in. I thought that people wouldn't accept witches but I was wrong. I've come here to say that I'm sorry about that rotten trick I played on you and I've brought your broomsticks back to prove it. And I wonder, could I please stay with you two?"

"Is this a trick, Maud?" asked Ethel suspiciously.

"No!" cried Maud. "I'm cold and I'm hungry and I'm lonely. You can see that I am."

"Then you'd better come and live with us here and help us with our work," said Mabel, smiling broadly. "We could do with some extra help. You see, Maud, they want us to take on a new service, called 'Meals on

Broomsticks'. We'll need an extra pair of hands and another broomstick if we're going to cope."

"Whatever is that?" demanded Maud.

"It's a service to deliver hot meals to people who find it hard to cook for themselves. It's usually called 'Meals on Wheels'. The problem is that by the time the meals have been carried up twenty flights of stairs they're cold. If we deliver them on our broomsticks, they'll still be all lovely and hot."

"Good," said Maud. "All I need is a good night's sleep and I'll be ready to go."

"You will be nice to people, won't you?" asked Ethel, looking worried. "You must promise not to scare them away."

"Maybe I will and maybe I won't. I'll just have to see if being good suits me as well as it suits you. Until I make up my mind, you'll just have to trust me, sisters dear."

However, Maud did very well. She flew around all day fetching and delivering and being every bit as pleasant as the other two. In fact, she became even more helpful than Ethel and Mabel, working till midnight and getting up first thing in the morning.

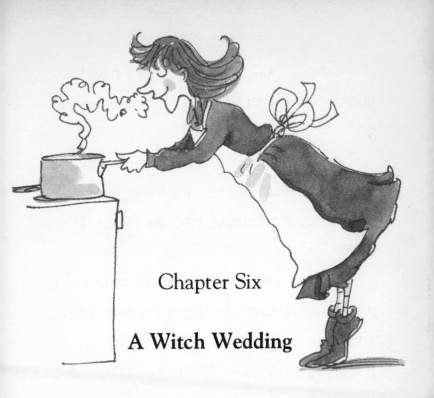

Chapter Six

A Witch Wedding

After a while Maud even began cooking special dishes for ill people: rice pudding and apple purée, beef broth and healthy chicken soup.

Her sisters didn't mind Maud cooking so long as she would leave them to sit in front of the television eating some

delicious take-away food. But Maud insisted that they help her, fetching and carrying, stirring, measuring and chopping.

Mabel and Ethel got so fed up they went round to see Gran.

"It's terrible," they burst out. "She makes us work all the time. We can't watch the television or listen to music or chat to our friends or sleep in late on Sundays. There's always something she makes us do."

"Oh, dear," said Gran, laughing. "She certainly is being good."

"You can say that again," groaned Mabel. "*And* she makes us say our prayers before we get into bed, even when it's very, very cold. It's just like it used to be when we were bad witches, being bossed about by Maud all the time."

"She even made us go to church *four* times last Sunday," added Mabel. "We like going to church. We always go to church now, but four times is a bit much."

"Oh, dear," agreed Gran. "I don't know what to suggest."

"I do," said Jackie. "The genius strikes again."

"All right, let's hear it," said Mabel. "Your last idea was a winner."

"Uncle Fred said she was a very

handsome woman," announced Jackie.

"So what?" moaned the witches.

"Fred!" exclaimed Gran. "My son Fred? Don't be daft. He's terrified of women. He never looks at them."

"Well, he looked at her," insisted Jackie. "Maybe they could get married."

"An excellent idea," agreed Gran. "I've wanted to see Fred married for years. I'll invite you all to dinner, and Fred too. Jackie, you, Lucy, Joe and your mum and dad must join us – so that it isn't too obvious. Next Saturday all right?"

"Yes," said Mabel, "but fancy Maud getting married. I can't imagine it."

"Bet you couldn't imagine her giving up being a bad witch, or turning into such a hard worker or you living in a flat and having friends. Isn't that right?"

"Yes," said Mabel, "but this is different. I mean, Maud was the wickedest witch I knew. And as for one of us getting married, well, I never even thought of it."

"It's worth a try," announced Ethel. "We've got nothing to lose and she's driving us round the bend at the moment."

"Umm," said Mabel, "I have an idea. How about a little love potion in their drinks? I think I remember enough spells to be able to do that. Let's have a

think. Ah yes, I think I remember:

Little potion in a tick,
Make the drinker lovesick.
They will sigh and moan and weep,
Until they find true love to keep."

"That's it!" cried Ethel. "Oh, Maud, you don't know what we're cooking up for you. Hee, hee! What fun!"

So the next Saturday they all arrived at Gran's flat. Maud was looking rather miserable because Ethel had put some of the potion in her tea in the morning and Mabel had put some in her coffee after lunch. There stood Maud, Ethel, Mabel, Jackie, Jackie's mum and dad and Lucy and Joe, with flowers and a bottle of wine and a box of chocolates, waiting for the door to be opened.

74

"Come on in," said Gran. "Oh, what lovely things! Are they for me? You are kind. Maud, you're looking lovely. I think you know everyone except my son, Fred."

Fred did not look very cheerful either. Ethel had been flying into his flat whenever he was out and putting the love potion on his toothbrush. But

he cheered up very quickly when he saw Maud and soon they were chatting away happily together.

By the end of the evening he was going to show her round the local museum and she had invited him to supper the following week.

To cut a long story short, the love potion worked very well and within two months the happy couple were engaged to be married.

"The only thing that worries me," Maud told her sisters, "is leaving you two in the lurch. I mean, it was kind of you to take me in after the trick I played on you. I feel bad about leaving you on your own."

"Don't give it a thought," Mabel assured her quickly. "Yes, we'll be sorry to lose you, Maud, of course we will, but we must think of your happiness. Just think how pleased dear Mother would have been. She was a married witch herself. She believed in marriage."

"Mother would have never forgiven us if we'd been selfish at a moment like this," added Ethel, biting her lip.

"You're right," agreed Maud. "We must do what Mother would have wished. I shall leave you the cauldron and the books. I am about to begin a new life. I shall go on working with you as before, of course, but other than that I shall forget all about witchcraft. Now, come on and help me choose a dress for the wedding."

Ethel whispered to Mabel, "Whew, that was a close thing! I thought for one terrible moment that she was going to stay with us."

"I know," agreed Mabel, "but we talked her out of it, thank goodness! After the wedding we'll be free again. Whoopee!"

When Jackie's mum and dad heard that Maud was going to marry Fred, they were very surprised.

"I'd completely given up on you, Fred," said Mum, giving him a big kiss.

"I'd given up on myself," laughed Fred, "but the first minute I saw Maud I knew she was the one."

"Congratulations, Fred," said Dad. "Great news."

So two weeks later Maud was married. It was much like any other wedding, except that the bride wore a long white dress with a witch's hat on her head and arrived on her broomstick with her two sisters.

After the ceremony there was a huge reception. All the people from the flats came and the local fast-food sellers all came too and gave the food for free. Everyone ate and ate and ate, pizzas and curry, Chinese food and kebabs, fish and chips and ice-cream. No one in the flats could remember when they had last had such a good time. When the time came for the happy couple to leave, Maud reached for her broom-stick, and yelled:

"Jump up behind, Fred."

Away they flew out of the window with Black Cat perched behind them, while everyone waved and threw confetti.

"I never thought to see my Fred married," wept Gran. "Ethel and Mabel, you've made an old woman very happy."

"Thank Jackie," said Ethel, "not us. It was all her idea."

"Right," agreed Jackie. "I'm a genius or maybe I'm a witch."

"Worse things you could be," said her gran.

"Umm, I think that's what I'll be when I grow up," Jackie told her. "A witch."

Everyone thought it was an excellent idea and there was a toast to Maud, the married witch; to Ethel and Mabel, the good witches; and to Jackie, the witch-to-be.